To my mum and dad, who took me to the library.

THE JINKS FAMILY
Me, Lucy, Mum, Dad and Stinky

Chapter 1

My hamster, Stinky, is usually pretty grumpy when he's just woken up. Or when he's tired. Or hungry.

Basically, he's in a bad mood quite a lot of the time.

Today, he lost his temper almost as soon as I got back from school.

'How was your day?' he asked me, which was nice enough.

'Pretty boring,' I said, sagging onto my bed.

'*Boring?!*' he spluttered, squinting at me

through the bars of his cage. 'Boring?!'

'A bit,' I said, shrugging. This made him twitch furiously.

'*I'm* stuck here all day,' he snapped, 'in this little hamster prison . . .'

'It's called a cage, Stinky.'

'In this cage on your desk, with absolutely nothing to do. Zero. Zilch.'

'You've got a little house to sleep in,' I pointed out. 'And you've got a wheel. You can always run on that.'

This seemed to annoy him even more.

'And why *on earth* would I want to do that? Going round and round and round all day, never actually getting anywhere? The only thing I've had to amuse me is this single piece of newspaper lining my cage. However,' he whinged, 'it's the sports page, and rodents in general aren't that interested in sport. Furthermore, even if I had wanted to read it, it's covered in my own poo, because someone –' he glared at me – 'hasn't cleaned it out for three days.'

3

He took a deep breath. 'And you're telling me that *your* day was boring?'

'Actually,' I said, 'if you must know, it wasn't all boring. Something *did* happen today. Something bad.' I sighed. 'Ty Hackett was pushing me around again.'

'Oh dear,' said Stinky, suddenly more sympathetic. 'That's becoming quite a hobby of his. What a horrible boy.'

Stinky had actually *met* Ty Hackett, which was pretty much when my problems started. I'd taken him into school, weeks ago, and he'd bitten Ty on the finger. Stinky had very sharp teeth for such a cute-looking animal.

Ty Hackett was the school bully, with a very small brain and really big fists.

'You should stand up to him,' Stinky said. 'Bullies don't like that.'

'He's almost twice my size,' I said.

'He's *seventeen* times *my* size,' Stinky explained, 'but that didn't stop *me* from chomping on his finger.'

'Even if I did stand up to him,' I said, 'he's got these two older brothers – twins – at high school and they're even bigger and meaner than him. They come back to our school a lot, to pick up Ty, and pick on everyone else. Do you really think it's a good idea to stand up to three Hacketts?'

But before Stinky could answer, my mum called my name from the kitchen. She was a normal-sized woman with a normal-sized voice – usually. But when she was  cross, or she had something important to say to me or my little sister, Lucy, her voice could get so loud that the house seemed to shake.

'**Benjamin Joseph Jinks!**
It's time to get ready ...
... we have to go in **ten** minutes!'

Stinky shuddered at the noise, and then frowned at me.

'Going?' he said. 'Going where?'

I sighed.

'It's Lucy. I have to go and watch her dancing in a show again. It's called *Very Happy Feet*. All the kids are going to be dressed up like penguins. We get free tickets because my mum makes the costumes.' I let out a huge sigh. 'Can you imagine, watching loads of little kids in penguin outfits, tap-dancing? It's going to be *so* boring.'

7

This started Stinky off on another rant of course.

'Boring? You don't know the meaning of the word. I'll be stuck in here again, by myself, with absolutely nothing to do. *Spy Gang*'s on tonight! And I'm going to miss it if you're not here to turn the TV on!'

Spy Gang was our all-time favourite TV show.

'I'll be back in time,' I said. 'I promise.'

And I *was* back in time.

But when I got home, my TV had gone.

Chapter 2

After the show, we piled out of the car and hurried up the front path, all of us happy to be home.

My dad, as usual, needed the toilet. My mum was desperate for a cup of tea. Lucy was exhausted after all that stomping around in a penguin suit. And I had to get to my room in time to watch *Spy Gang* with Stinky.

My mum went to put the key in the lock, but the door was already open.

Instead of us all rushing off in different

directions, we stood on the doorstep, gawping into the house.

It wasn't what we *could* see that stopped us in our tracks. It was what we *couldn't* see. No clock. No TV. Lots of other things were missing

too. My mum gasped. Lucy shrieked. My dad was the first to speak.

'We've been burgled,' he muttered. Then he told us to move away from the door a bit, just to be safe. 'Wait there.'

He stepped carefully into the house, and went briskly from room to room to make sure no one was still in there. When he came back, he said, 'They're gone. And so,' he added with a sigh, 'is a lot of our stuff.'

My mum was hugging Lucy very tightly indeed.

'I'll call the police,' she said quietly.

I burst into the house, dashed to my room, flung open my door and sighed with relief: Stinky was still there in his cage. But apart from my bed and the desk and the wardrobe, everything else was gone: my games console, my toys, my TV.

'Welcome home,' Stinky said as I slumped onto the bed.

'What happened?'

'Some aliens came and beamed everything up.'

'Really?'

'No,' he said. 'Blimey. Of course not. Aliens indeed. You've had

burglars. And, what is more, I know who they are.'

I gasped.

'It happened just after you left,' he continued. 'I was in my house, having a nap, when I heard these two voices and so I poked my head out. Two older kids. Big. Very big. One of them was carrying your TV. The other one had most of your other stuff in a box.'

'And what did you do?'

'Do?' he said. '*Do?* What do you think I did? Am I a guard-hamster? Is there a "Beware of the Hamster" sign on the front door? I just stayed quiet, of course. But here's the thing –

one of them spotted me. He said, "Hey, there's the hamster that bit Ty," and the other one laughed.'

'Ty? They knew Ty Hackett?'

'Not only knew him, but looked like him too.'

Stinky waited impatiently for the penny to drop.

'*His brothers?*' I said. 'The twins?'

He nodded.

'So,' I said, 'let's tell the police.'

'Tell them what, exactly? "Yes, officer, my *hamster* can identify the burglars"?'

'Didn't think of that,' I admitted.

I couldn't even tell my mum and dad what Stinky had seen – they just thought he was a regular hamster. They had no idea that he was a genius, and that's the way that Stinky wanted it.

'But what can we do? We can't let them get away with it, can we?'

'You said they still come back to your school sometimes.'

'Yes. To pick up Ty, or just to hang around and make trouble.'

'So what we need is *surveillance*.'

'Serve-whatty?'

'Snooping. Like they do in *Spy Gang*. Watching the Hacketts to see what they get up to. Trying to find out where they're going to break in next, and calling the police to tip them off.'

'I thought you were *terrified* of being outside,' I said. 'But you'd still be happy following them?'

'Not me, you dimwit. *You.*'

Chapter 3

Being a spy looks really cool on TV. It *isn't*. It's just hours and hours of waiting and waiting, sprinkled with little bits of absolute terror.

Like now.

I pushed my back tight against the tree. The binoculars were trembling in my hand.

The tree was only a tiny bit wider than me but it was all that hid me from the Hackett twins. They were leaning against the school wall, only a pebble's throw away from me.

I'd been trying to watch them for weeks and weeks, and this was the closest I'd ever got and the most afraid I'd ever been.

There was no one else around. School had finished half an hour ago and my bag was heavy with homework from my horrible teacher, Mr McCreedy.

The sky was all murky. A storm was coming, but if the Hacketts spotted me, that would be the least of my problems. They'd pummel me to a pulp. They'd bash me to bits. They'd squash me like a satsuma. I ducked my head back out of sight.

The binoculars were my dad's. He used to take them to the racetrack so he could get a better look at his horses losing. 'What do you need them for?' he'd asked me. 'Birdwatching,' I'd told him.

Also in my school bag was the camera I'd borrowed from my mum. I'd told her that it *was* for birdwatching too. She'd frowned at me. 'That's a nice peaceful hobby,' she'd said doubtfully.

Now I nervously poked my head out from the tree to see what the twins were up to. They were waiting for something, I was sure about that. I didn't know what. But I planned to find out.

They were identical, as far as I could tell. The same freckled skin. The same mean little piggy eyes. And the same massive fists to mash me like a potato if they caught me spying.

Someone was marching over to them and I didn't need the binoculars to work out who it was.

Old. Bald. Huge beard.

Beardy McCreedy!

I was afraid of the Hackett twins, but my teacher scared me more. He was mean, unpleasant and he hated kids.

I'd thought that he was going to tell the twins off, but that wasn't it. As I peered through the binoculars, I saw that McCreedy was actually *smiling*. It looked strange on his face, the smile, like it didn't belong there.

He was clutching a blue plastic folder and he pulled out a piece of paper with a flourish. There was writing but I couldn't make it out.

I stuffed the binoculars into my bag and grabbed the camera. And when McCreedy handed one of them the paper, I snapped a picture.

Big mistake.

Big, big mistake.

It was so cloudy and dark that the flash from my camera went off. I ducked behind the tree again.

My mouth was suddenly dry and my legs were all wobbly.

I didn't know if they'd seen me but they must have seen the flash, and they'd surely come looking.

What could I do? If I ran, they'd see me and catch me. So I stayed behind the tree and hoped they'd somehow missed it. All the while, I was waiting for a hand to reach around and grab me. I felt like an animal caught in a trap.

I could hardly breathe. I heard footsteps coming towards me, and mumbled voices.

Just then came a gigantic flash of lightning, illuminating the whole sky. Seconds later, an enormous crackle of thunder, and then rain

came tumbling down.

Maybe I was saved! The flash from my camera might have looked like lightning! And maybe the twins had run off to shelter from the storm. But I didn't dare peek.

Never stay under a tree in a thunderstorm, said a voice in my head, but it was a long time before I risked looking out. I did it very slowly, holding my breath.

26

No one was there! My body tingled with relief.

The rain was fast and noisy, bouncing off the ground. I was going to get absolutely drenched. But I ran home anyway. I couldn't wait to tell Stinky what I'd seen.

Chapter 4

Later that night, Stinky was pacing up and down my desk while I cleaned his cage. I screwed up the old piece of newspaper, put down a fresh sheet, then scooped Stinky up and put him back.

'Careful,' he snapped. 'I'm not a stuffed toy, you know.'

'I know you're not,' I replied. 'Stuffed toys don't poo half as much.'

We were both really tetchy. I was tetchy because of the close shave I'd had with

Beardy and the Hacketts. Stinky was tetchy because my sister had sneaked in to play with him while I was out spying. She loved hugging him and dressing him up in her dolls' clothes. Stinky didn't like either of those things. 'Hamsters – especially boy hamsters – are not meant to wear dresses,' he'd grumbled as soon as I'd got home.

'And when she hugs me, it's like I'm being *choked*.'

To take his mind off my sister, I cleaned his cage and told him what I'd seen on my spying mission.

'It's pretty strange, isn't it?' I said. 'McCreedy meeting the twins like that to give them information.'

'Very suspicious indeed. And I suppose you know that other kids at your school have been burgled too?'

'No,' I said. 'How do *you* know that?'

He pointed a paw towards the scrunched-up newspaper.

'It was under my nose,' he said. 'And under my poo actually, in the paper. Three burglaries in two weeks – and they were all houses of kids at your school.'

'And you think Beardy was involved?'

'More than involved!' he exclaimed. 'I think he's some kind of master criminal. He's getting those boys to break into houses for him. He tells them where to go.'

'But how does he choose the houses? And how does he know they'll be empty?'

Stinky shook his head.

'That's the question,' he said.

We both fell quiet for a minute, thinking. But it was me that had the idea this time.

'That's it!' I said. 'It's been under *my* nose all this time. Of course!'

'I beg your pardon?'

'Maybe something's been under my nose all this time. I knew I'd seen a blue folder somewhere else. He's got a briefcase, and he keeps it open beside his feet in class. And there's always a blue folder in there.'

Stinky's eyes lit
up.

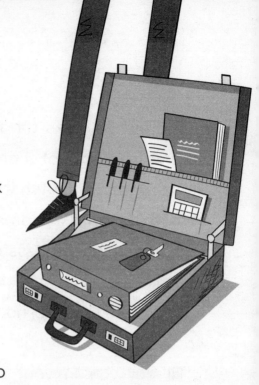

'So have a quick
flick through it
tomorrow when
he's not looking,'
he said.

'Are you crazy?
I'd never be able to
do it. There are all the other kids in the class
for a start. And McCreedy has eyes like an
owl. If somebody blinks, he knows about it.
There's no way I could find out what's in that
folder without him seeing me.'

'What about at lunchtime?' Stinky asked.
'Does he take the briefcase with him?'

'No, but he locks the room and makes sure we're all out of there.' Then I had an amazing thought. 'What I really need is something small – something small and furry – to stay in the classroom at lunchtime and take a look.'

'Oh no,' he said. 'No, no, no. Definitely not. *Absolutely, positively* not.'

'I'll put you in your special lunchbox, the one with breathing holes,' I explained excitedly. 'I'll put the box in my bag, and leave the bag in the classroom at lunchtime. When no one's there, you'll wriggle out of the bag, go over to his briefcase and climb in to see what's in the folder. Then you'll scurry back to my bag and into the lunchbox, and

the mission will be accomplished.'

'No, it won't,' he said, shaking his head. 'Because I won't be there. I'll be here, safe and sound.'

'Come on, Stinky – what can possibly go wrong?'

'A lot,' he said. 'An awful lot.'

'*I'll* be taking care of you.'

'That's what I'm worried about,' he mumbled.

'All right, then,' I said, shrugging, pretending not to care. 'Have it your way. Oh – did I tell you that Lucy's got the day off school tomorrow? She'll probably be in here all day, playing with you, dressing you up, giving you hugs. You'll have loads of fun.'

Stinky went quiet for ages.

'OK,' he said eventually. 'I'm coming.'

Then he climbed onto his wheel and started running. It was something he only ever did

when he was feeling *really* stressed. Tonight
he was on there for hours.

Chapter 5

It was time.

When the bell rang for lunch, I took a deep breath.

As all the other kids scraped back their chairs, stood up and headed for the door, I reached into my bag, opened my lunchbox, and whispered, 'Good luck,' to Stinky.

I was the last one to leave.

McCreedy was waiting by the door with the key in his hand, tapping his foot impatiently and scowling at me.

'Come on!' he barked. 'Get a move on, boy! I've known faster *snails*.'

When I was finally out of the classroom, he grunted, locked the door and hurtled off in the direction of the staffroom, muttering to himself.

Everyone else in my class had gone outside or to the lunch room, but I was far too nervous to play or to eat. I stood in the corridor, right next to the door, worrying about Stinky.

Had he struggled out of my bag yet? Where was he now? We'd had a practice last night and he'd managed to wriggle out. But maybe today would be different. Maybe he would be too exhausted after being on his wheel most of last night, and he wouldn't get out.

inside bag

Maybe he would be out of breath after the journey from my bag to McCreedy's desk, and be stranded in the middle of the classroom.

Maybe he wouldn't be able to climb into the

briefcase, or maybe he'd get in there but not be able to escape, like a spider trapped in a bath. That would be the worst thing. He'd be stuck in the briefcase and Beardy would take him home, and then *who knew* what would happen?

Because I couldn't see what he was doing now, I was imagining the worst.

The more I thought about it, the queasier I became.

When lunchtime was almost over, I hardly noticed that the other kids had come back and were waiting by the door.

Even when Ty Hackett strolled over, barged into me and then stood right in front of me, glaring and muttering threats, I wasn't worried for my own safety. I was just thinking about my brave hamster, risking his life on the other side of the door.

And then Ty Hackett slunk away, because the stumpy figure of McCreedy was striding towards us, the key in his hand and a grimace on his face.

'Out of my way!' Beardy snapped at any kids who were standing in his path.

I stepped to the side to let him past.

But when he flung open the door, I was the first one in.

Chapter 6

I rushed straight to my seat and looked in my bag. A wave of relief surged through my body. Stinky was there in the lunchbox, panting heavily.

I didn't know if the mission had been successful, but he was safe, and that was the most important thing. I smiled at him and then zipped up my bag.

When the class was full and everyone was sitting down, Beardy cleared his throat to get our attention. It was like a horrible rumble of thunder.

'We are going to do some writing,' he boomed. 'Today's assignment is to write about the most valuable thing in your house. Explain *what* it is, *why* it is valuable and *where* it is.' He scribbled 'what', 'why' and 'where' on the board and then he glared at us. 'Well?' he said. 'What are you all waiting for?'

I sat there for a while, trying to calm down,

and trying to think of what I could possibly write about. There wasn't much valuable left in our house.

Apart from Stinky of course.

Maybe he was reading my thoughts, because at that moment a noise came from my bag. At first it was very faint tap-tapping, but it got louder and louder. When it didn't stop, I whispered '*sh**hh**'* and the kids nearby gave me funny looks. Well, I *was* shushing my schoolbag. But the bag refused to be quiet, and now Beardy was scowling in my direction.

I coughed. At first it was only to cover up the tapping noise, but then I worried that Stinky was in trouble – maybe he'd been hurt on his spying mission. So I kept coughing, hoping

 that McCreedy would order me to leave the room. My throat started hurting. Everyone was looking, and a few kids started giggling nervously.

McCreedy grimaced. He was so annoyed that his face – or at least the part not hidden by his beard – was turning a deep shade of pink. It made me think of the time that McCreedy had lost a bet to my dad, and – despite my fear – a giggle caught in my throat, making me splutter more.

'Go and get a drink of water, boy!' he yelled. 'Now!'

I snatched up my bag, still coughing and wheezing all the time, and staggered out of the class, with everyone giggling behind me. As I raced down the corridor, I heard Beardy bellow an almighty **'SHUSH!'** to the class.

Chapter 7

In the safety of a toilet cubicle, I unzipped my bag and opened up the lunchbox. Stinky blinked up at me and hopped onto my open palm.

'What's up?' I said, panting. 'You OK?'

'I'm fine, thanks for asking,' he said calmly.

'So what was all that tapping about, then?' I asked, feeling annoyed.

'I needed to tell you what I found.'

'And it couldn't have waited until after class?' I asked him.

'Oh no.'

'Go on then – what was in the folder?'

'Homework,' he announced.

'Homework?'

'Homework.'

'You made me come here for *that*? I faked a coughing fit and had Beardy yelling at me and everyone laughing at me – *again* – for *that*? *Of course he's got homework*. He's a teacher, Stinky.'

'But that homework explains *everything*,' said Stinky.

I looked at him blankly.

'Do you remember when I had to help you describe your house for your homework?' he said. 'And then another time you had to write about something you were going to do with your whole family, and you wrote about going to watch your sister in the penguin show. And now, as we're talking, the entire class is writing about something in their house that's valuable. Do you see? He uses the information he gets from his students. He already knows where everyone lives from the school records. And now from all the kids' writing he knows what the houses are like and when they'll be empty. Then the Hackett twins do the job for him.'

I gasped.

'You always wondered,' Stinky continued, 'why someone who hated kids so much would be a teacher. Well, now we have one good reason – he's doing it to arrange burglaries.'

'So let's go to the police,' I whispered.

Stinky shook his head.

'And you think they'll believe a nine-year-old who says his teacher is a criminal mastermind?'

I saw Stinky's point.

'No – I have a better idea. What were you going to write about in class? The most valuable thing in your house?'

'You, probably,' I said. He stared at me.

'What?' he spluttered. 'Have you totally lost your . . . ?'

'Relax, relax. I'm going to leave out the stuff about you talking and being a genius and all that. I'm going to pretend you're just a normal hamster who sleeps a lot and poos a lot. And

I wouldn't be making it up about the sleeping and the pooing.'

He sighed.

'Why don't you write about something else?' he said.

'For example?'

'A huge diamond.'

'But we don't have a . . .' I started, but then I understood his plan. 'That's *good*. We pretend

that we have something dead expensive and then the Hackett twins come back to our house to steal it.'

'And also tell him a time when the house is empty. And then we'll set a trap.'

'Monday night,' I said. 'Lucy's got another concert.'

Stinky nodded.

'I can tell you what to write,' he said, but I shook my head.

'It's time I did my own work,' I told him. 'I can do it.'

I put him back in the box, and the box in my bag, and then I rushed back to class. McCreedy scowled again as I sat down at my desk. This is what I wrote:

The Most Valuable Thing in My House

by Ben Jinks

My mum has this incredible diamond necklace. The necklace is pure gold and the diamond is as big as my thumb, and  very sparkly. She hardly ever wears it though. It's worth too much money, she says. It was left to her by my Great-Aunt Cecilia, and all the other relatives were jealous.

It's sticky-taped to the bottom of the bed in my mum and dad's room, because my dad says that burglars would never think of looking there.

Me and my sister aren't allowed to even touch it. My sister Lucy really wanted to wear it for a dance show about fairies she's doing next Monday evening, but my mum said no, so Lucy has to do the show without it. We're all going to watch it.

Now all that was left for Stinky and me to do was wait and see if our plan worked.

Chapter 8

On Monday evening it was cold, but Stinky was sweating from all the running he was doing on his wheel. We were waiting nervously for my family to leave and could hear the usual commotion downstairs – Lucy shouting at Mum about her costume and Dad running off to the loo.

Finally the front door clicked shut behind them and Stinky hopped off his wheel, tried to get his breath back and wheezed, 'Let's do it.'

I'd already done the first bit of the plan –

getting out of watching Lucy's show. It had been easier than I'd thought.

The venue was only three minutes' drive away, and Mum had decided that, for the first time ever, I could be trusted to stay home alone. I think she was relieved not to take me, to be honest, after I'd fidgeted all through the last show, the penguin one.

Dad had offered to stay home with me, but hadn't been so lucky. He left his spare phone with me though, and said to text him if there was a problem of any kind; he was definitely looking for any excuse to get out of another hour and a half of tap-dancing.

The next stage of our plan was to booby-trap my mum and dad's room, to slow the

burglars down. There was no time to lose. The Hackett twins could be here at any moment. I emptied a box of drawing pins under my parents' bed and spread them out, pointy side up. After that, I bounded onto the bed, stood on tiptoe and unscrewed the lightbulb.

Then I left the room and dashed out of the house, into the back garden. To the shed.

It was full of bags and boxes of stuff we were supposedly going to get rid of one day in a big garage sale, as well as old costumes my mum had made for Lucy's shows. I found what I was looking for, grabbed it and rushed out to Stinky.

It was a baby monitor. When Lucy was little, my mum and dad used to leave the

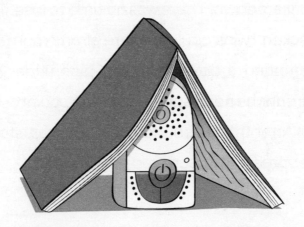

microphone bit by her cot and put the speaker in the living room. That way they could watch the telly and still hear her crying.

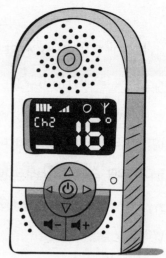

I plugged in the microphone and hid it under an open book next to the cage.

The final part of the plan was for me to go back to the shed and hide. Stinky would use the baby monitor to whisper to me that they were in the house, and I'd call the police.

'Do you have the phone?' Stinky asked. I nodded.

I took a final look at Stinky.

'You seem twitchy,' I said.

'I'm a hamster,' he said. 'We twitch. But I'm quite OK. It's you that seems particularly worried in fact,' he added.

'I'm a human,' I said. 'We worry. That's what we do.'

'It's time for you to go, Ben,' he said.

I nodded again. 'Good luck.'

In the shed, the speaker from the baby monitor was on the floor, ready. I turned it on and looked down at it. At first I couldn't keep still. I was jumpy with excitement.

I tried to settle into waiting quietly.

Then I got impatient.

And then, after a long time with nothing at

all happening. I started to feel really cold. It was *freezing*. I could see my breath in the air.

The shed was as cold as a polar bear's bottom, if not colder.

I hopped from foot to foot to get warm, but it was no use. I started to shiver. If I had to wait much longer, I'd turn blue.

I looked around for something to wear. There were bags and boxes of my old toys – cars, toy guns, some teddies – but all our old clothes had gone to Oxfam a few months ago.

Then I spotted the big bag of penguin outfits that my mum had made for Lucy's last show. I rummaged through it. Most of the costumes were too small, but there was one tall-ish girl in Lucy's dance group and I put hers on. I felt a bit silly of course. It's hard *not* to feel silly when you're dressed up like a penguin. But I was a lot warmer now.

And then I sat down and waited for a sound – any sound – from the speaker.

And the more I waited, the more I realised how rubbish the plan was after all.

I mean, maybe they wouldn't come and I'd be spending hours in a shed, in a penguin costume, for nothing.

Or – worse – they *would* come, see that the diamond wasn't under the bed, steal what little was left after their first visit and get away before the police could get here. Then I'd have to try and explain it all to my family. Where would I start?

But then I heard a faint crackle from the speaker. And a familiar voice I could just make out.

'Call the police!' Stinky whispered.

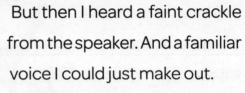

They're here!

Chapter 9

I quickly texted Dad – 'Come home now' – then called the police. After that, all I could do was wait again and listen as Stinky told me what was happening.

'They're in your parents' room now,' he whispered. 'They went straight there. They're trying to turn the light on and complaining about the dark . . . Now they're arguing about who should have brought a torch.'

There was a few seconds' quiet, until I

heard yelping in the background and Stinky sniggering.

'They're both being jabbed by the drawing pins under the bed. Oh, this is even better than I thought it would be! And now it sounds very much like they're groping about in the dark and realising that the diamond isn't there. They're squealing in pain as they try to get out from

under the bed. Now they're coming out of your parents' room.' Stinky lowered his voice even more. 'They're going to look under the beds in the other rooms. Right, someone's coming –'

And then I heard nothing for a while. It was torture. I wondered how much longer the police would take.

The next voice I heard was one of the twins.

'Nothing here. What a stupid waste of time. We already took all the stuff that's worth taking.'

'Maybe not,' said the other one. 'I've got an idea. Let's play a trick on Ty. We'll take that hamster that bit him and put it in his lunchbox when he's not looking.'

The other twin laughed. 'That's good,' he said. 'Let's grab it and get out of here.'

I felt a cold shiver.

And then I froze completely when I heard the next voice.

'Get your hand out of the cage . . .'

Or I'll bite it off!

Stinky said. A silence followed – it seemed to go on forever. I was staring at the speaker so hard that I forgot to breathe.

'He spoke. The – the – that hamster *spoke.*'

'I'll do more than speak, dimwit, if you don't scram. I know who you are, Hacketts, and I'll do worse to you than I did to your brother, you wait and see. I know everything – about McCreedy and all the other burglaries. Everything. And if you don't do what I say, you'll be in trouble. *Big* trouble.'

There was another silence. It was quiet for so long that I thought the speaker had broken, or that the twins had been shocked speechless. But when one of them finally spoke, his voice was like ice.

'That hamster knows too much,' he said. 'Kill it!'

I gasped.

I had to do something and didn't have time to think.

I grabbed a toy gun and sprinted into the house.

It's not easy, running in a penguin costume. When I burst into my room, I was panting heavily.

Both of the Hackett twins spun around and stared at me. One of them had his hand in the cage groping around for Stinky. When I pointed the toy gun at him, he looked as if he'd seen a ghost.

I said, in the deepest voice I could manage:

He pulled his hand out of the cage.

Stinky was shaking with relief.

'And stay out,' he spluttered.

'A – a – a talking hamster and a talking penguin,' the other twin said. I pointed the toy gun at *him* now. 'Don't shoot me, penguin,' he pleaded. 'I promise we'll never be bad to animals again. We promise. We promise. Don't we?'

He looked at his brother, who opened his mouth to speak, but no sound came out.

I don't know who was more terrified – the twins, or me and Stinky.

I was worried they'd soon work out that I wasn't a huge talking penguin but a kid trembling inside a costume.

'Mr – Mr Penguin,' stuttered the second twin. 'How? How do you know everything?'

I didn't know how to answer. But Stinky did.

'We've been watching you,' he said. 'We've got friends in high places. Birds, for one. Squirrels, for another. Cats. A huge network of

animal informants. And if you don't tell the police everything – about the burglaries and McCreedy – we'll *keep on* watching you. *Wherever you go.*'

The twins looked very pale. It was like they wanted to get away, more than anything else in the world, but they didn't dare move.

Then I heard our car: the exhaust was noisy and unmistakable. Dad was home! Right after that we heard the police siren. I sighed with relief, then told the twins to put their hands up and walk very slowly out of the room and out of the house. They did.

'Toodle-oo,' said Stinky.

And that was the last we saw of them.

Chapter 10

'So you were doing your homework when the burglars burst in?' my dad said, with a very puzzled expression. 'And they were so shocked to see someone home, they just went back out the front door – where the police were waiting?'

I nodded.

The police had left, Mum and Lucy had come back after the concert, and all the family were crammed into my bedroom. Dad was pacing up and down. My mum was sitting on the bed, hugging me and promising not to leave me alone again until I was at least twenty-one. Lucy was sitting at the desk, frowning. She'd spotted something under my bed.

'What's that penguin costume doing there?' she asked. 'And what have you been doing with the baby monitor?'

'Also,' said my dad, who was looking even more bamboozled, 'the police said there were drawing pins under our bed. Lots of them.'

Everyone was waiting for an explanation.

I was straining to think of a story that could somehow explain everything, and yet not get me into trouble.

But then I looked at my mum and dad

and Lucy, and I gave up trying.

It wears you out, telling lies all the time.

So I took a deep breath.

'The truth is,' I said, eventually, 'we set a trap for the burglars tonight.'

'We?' said my dad.

'Me and my hamster.'

They all stared at me. For ages.

My dad could hardly get his words out.

'You – you set a trap? You – and . . .'

'Stinky, here. He's a bit of a genius.'

'A bit of a genius?'

'A lot of a genius.'

'And you know he's a genius because . . . ?'

'He talks.'

'He *talks*? In *English*?' my dad said.

'And French actually. Come on, Stinky, say something.'

Now everyone was staring at him, but he was twitching in the corner of his cage, looking exactly like a regular hamster. And saying nothing at all.

My mum, hugging me tighter now, whispered to my dad, 'Call the doctor, Derek.'

'No, no, Mum. I'm OK. Really. I can explain. It was like this – I was in the shed in the penguin outfit, and Stinky was telling me what was happening – on the baby monitor.'

My mum stroked my hair. 'There, there, Ben. Mummy's here. It'll be OK. You've just had a nasty fright, that's all. Burglars in the house – it's enough to give anyone a shock.'

'I'm telling the truth, Mum. Honest. Tell them, Stinky. *Say something*.' But Stinky stayed silent. 'He must be traumatised or something.'

'*Someone's* traumatised,' my dad muttered sadly.

'*Stinky!*' I pleaded. 'Tell them!'

But Stinky just looked blankly back at me.

My mum hugged me so tight I could hardly breathe, and Lucy looked like she didn't know whether to laugh or cry.

'That's it,' my dad announced. 'I'm calling the doctor.'

'Don't!' I begged him, and then I took a deep breath. '*OK*. Sorry. Mum's right. Maybe I just need to rest.'

Dad sighed with relief.

'Good lad,' he said. 'Come on, Lucy – let's give your brother a bit of space.'

My sister was speechless. She took one more look at the penguin costume, then at me, and finally at Stinky, shaking her head, until my dad led her away.

Mum tucked me into bed and stroked my head until I pretended to be asleep.

When she left and closed the door behind her, I sat up.

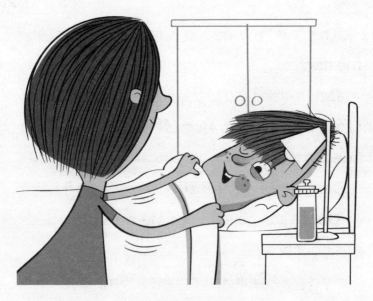

'Thanks a lot, Stinky,' I whispered. 'Now my family all think I've lost my mind.'

'*You must have,*' he snapped. 'Why else would you tell them about me? Do you *really* think they're capable of keeping a secret? Your sister would tell the whole school in five minutes flat and I'd be in all the newspapers and on the TV and then scientists would take me away to perform horrible experiments on my brain and . . .'

'All right, all right,' I whispered. 'Calm down.'

We glared at each other for a very long time.

Eventually I said, 'We did a good job tonight though, didn't we, Stinky?'

And it was then that I think he actually smiled.

'The best,' he said. 'The best.'

Chapter 11

After Beardy was sent to jail, and the twins were sent away to a centre for naughty kids, the police gave us back all our stolen things, including my old TV.

Straight after tea tonight, I raced to my room as usual to put the TV back on for Stinky. It always made  him happy. He watched a lot of television, for a hamster.

There was a documentary about deer on tonight and we watched it together. Stinky was a big fan of wildlife shows. They made him feel really good about himself.

'There are some breathtakingly stupid animals out there.' He jabbed a paw at the screen. 'Take deer, for example – absolutely no common sense. And don't get me started on rabbits.' Then he turned away from the TV for a moment to look at me. 'How was school today, by the way?'

'Pretty good,' I said. I knew better than to tell him it was 'boring' by now.

'What was pretty good?' Stinky asked. 'Give me details.'

'Well, my new teacher's really nice. And Ty Hackett's gone very quiet since his brothers were sent away.'

Stinky smiled.

'I have a feeling that those twins are actually happy to be there,' he said.

'Happy to be locked up?' I said, raising my eyebrows.

'Well,' he explained, 'if you thought that a huge network of talking animals was watching your every move, perhaps you'd prefer to be indoors too.'

He had a point.

After the wildlife documentary finished, we watched a quiz show (Stinky always got the answers before the contestants) and then it was time for *Spy Gang*. It was still our all-time favourite.

We'd only been watching it for a few minutes when my dad poked his head into the room.

'You're not watching this rubbish on the telly again, are you, Ben?' he said, with a chuckle. 'Honestly, it's so far-fetched. This kind of thing could never happen in real life.'

Then he left and closed the door behind him.

'That's what he thinks,' I whispered to Stinky, and we both grinned.

THE END

Have you read the first
STINKY and JINKS
adventure?

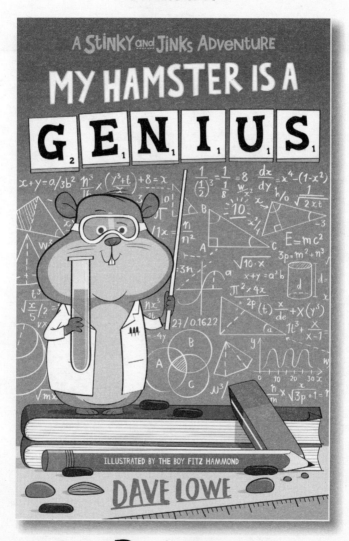

Look out for more
STINKY and JINKS
adventures...

A Stinky and Jinks Adventure

MY HAMSTER IS AN

ASTRONAUT

DAVE LOWE

ILLUSTRATED BY
THE BOY FITZ HAMMOND

Piccadilly
PRESS

A STINKY and JINKS ADVENTURE

MY HAMSTER'S GOT
TALENT

DAVE LOWE

ILLUSTRATED BY
THE BOY FITZ HAMMOND

Piccadilly
PRESS

Dave Lowe grew up in Dudley in the West Midlands, and now lives in Brisbane, Australia, with his wife and two daughters. He spends his days writing books, drinking lots of tea, and treading on Lego that his daughters have left lying around. Dave's Stinky and Jinks books follow the adventures of a nine-year-old boy called Ben, and Stinky, Ben's genius pet hamster. (When Dave was younger, he had a pet hamster too. Unlike Stinky, however, Dave's hamster didn't often help him with his homework.) Find Dave online at @daveloweauthor or www.davelowebooks.com

Born in York in the late 1970s, **The Boy Fitz Hammond** now lives in Edinburgh with his wife and their two sons. A freelance illustrator for well over a decade, he loves to draw in a variety of styles, allowing him to work on a range of projects across all media. Find him online at www.nbillustration.co.uk/the-boy-fitz-hammond or on Twitter @tbfhDotCom

PRESS

Thank you for choosing a Piccadilly Press book.

If you would like to know more about our authors, our books or if you'd just like to know what we're up to, you can find us online.

www.piccadillypress.co.uk

You can also find us on:

We hope to see you soon!